Pete the Cat

Robo-Pete

by James Dean

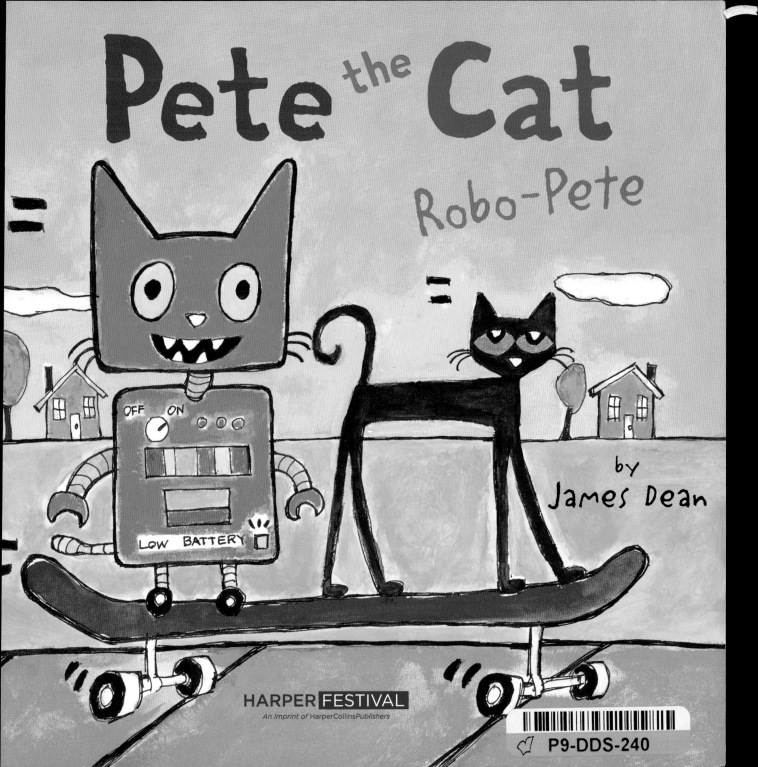

HARPER FESTIVAL
An Imprint of HarperCollinsPublishers

HarperFestival is an imprint of HarperCollins Publishers.

Pete the Cat: Robo-Pete
Copyright © 2015 by James Dean. All rights reserved.
Manufactured in China.

For information address HarperCollins Children's Books, a division of HarperCollins Publishers,
195 Broadway, New York, NY 10007.
www.harpercollinschildrens.com
Library of Congress Control Number: 2015936663
ISBN 978-0-06-230427-8

Book design by Jeanne Hogle
15 16 17 18 19   LEO   10 9 8 7 6 5 4 3 2 1
❖
First Edition

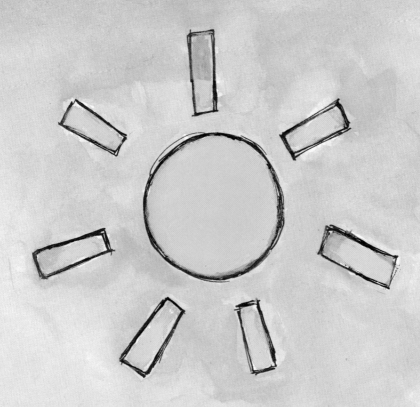

What a great, sunny morning! Pete can't wait to play baseball with his friends.

"Do you want to play catch?"
Pete asks Larry.
"I can't," says Larry.
"I'm going to the library."

"Do you want to play catch?"
Pete asks Callie.
"I was about to go for a
bike ride," says Callie.

"Do you want to play catch?" Pete asks John.
"I can't right now," says John. "I have to paint the fence."

Pete wishes his friends would do
what he wants to do. It's no fun
playing catch all by himself.
If only I knew another me . . . ,
Pete thinks. And like that,
Pete has a great idea!

Pete builds a robot! He programs it to be just like him.

"Welcome to the world, Robo-Pete!" Pete says to the robot.
"You're my new best friend. We'll do everything together."

"And I want to play catch," says Pete.
"Great idea!" says Robo-Pete.

Pete and Robo-Pete play catch.

"Wow!" says Pete, running after the ball. "You sure can throw far!"

Robo-Pete throws farther and farther until . . .

"Time out!" says Pete as he tries to catch his breath.
"Let's play something else."
"I want to play whatever you want to play,"
Robo-Pete says proudly.

"How about we play hide-and-seek?" says Pete.
"That will be fun," says Robo-Pete.

Pete finds the best hiding place ever! He's sure Robo-Pete will never find him.

"Ten, nine, eight, seven, six, five, four, three, two, one!" shouts Robo-Pete. "Ready or not, here I come!"

"Gotcha!" shouts Robo-Pete, tagging Pete.
"Hey, how did you find me?" says Pete.
"With my homing device," says Robo-Pete.
"I can find anyone, anywhere."

"Okay, enough hide-and-seek," says Pete. "Let's play some guitar."

Pete teaches Robo-Pete how to play a song he made up.

"You have to feel the music,"
Pete explains.
"Okay," says Robo-Pete.

"To feel it, I need to play loud," explains Robo-Pete.

Pete tries to stop Robo-Pete, but Robo-Pete can't hear him over the noise. . . .

"This is fun," says Robo-Pete.

"This is awful!" says Pete the Cat.

"Okay," says Robo-Pete. "Let's ride our skateboards instead."

Before Pete can answer, Robo-Pete's feet transform into a motorized skateboard with super speedy wheels.

"Let's go!"

Robo-Pete shouts.

"Wait!" calls Pete.

Pete chases after Robo-Pete. He has no idea where Robo-Pete is going.

Robo-Pete crashes into the sandbox at the playground.
"Are you okay?" Pete asks his robot.

"I am a robot. I am indestructible!" says Robo-Pete.
"What is this strange place?"
"It's a playground," says Pete. He waves to his friends.

"This is Robo-Pete," Pete says to Callie, Larry, and John.
"I made him myself."
"Cool," says Larry.

"We are going to help John finish painting," says Callie.
"And then we are going bike riding."
"I want to go on the slide!" interrupts Robo-Pete.

"Robo-Pete, I want to help my friends paint the fence!"
Pete tells his robot.

"Paint the fence—that would be great," Robo-Pete says.
"I am programmed to paint faster than anyone."

Pete and his friends try to help, but Robo-Pete paints too fast.

So instead they ride bikes,

and they read books . . .

and after Robo-Pete is done painting,
they help him clean the brushes.

Pete realizes that it doesn't matter what they do.
Just being with his friends is what makes it fun!